This Book Belongs To

DONKEY SAVES CHRISTMAS

Written by Dave Thorne
Illustrated by Kris Lillyman

Farmers have such busy days, there's always things to do
With milking cows, and herding sheep, and feeding piggies too
The best job of the year to do – as Farmer liked to say
Was getting set for everyone to come on Christmas day.

Christmas day upon the farm was happy and quite loud
With all the family coming round, there's really quite a crowd
Their parents and their Aunty Maud – who always made it jolly
Four brothers and eight nephews; and the farmers Uncle Wally.

With oh so many things to do
- and so much to remember.
They made sure that
the tree went up
- the first day
of December.

They put on tinsel and some lights - and a fairy on as well.
Then paper chains, a few nice stars - and a shiny Christmas bell.

They did the house, and then the barn, and then the garden shed
And Donkey wore a funny hat - with antlers on his head
They even had a big red sleigh – that came out every year
And everywhere you looked you'd see a lot of Christmas cheer

The Turkeys had escaped by then - as always in December
They always checked the calendar - so no need to remember
The chickens and the geese had gone - all hiding in the hay
Though everyone turned up again - when it was Christmas day

The snow came down on Christmas Eve – a very heavy storm
They had to go and fetch the cows – to get them in the warm
They found the cows all shivering – while hiding under trees
The snow still getting deeper – til it came up to their knees

But when the farmer left the house, he hadn't shut the door
He really hadn't meant to – and he'd not done it before
The problem wasn't just the cold – the house would still be cosy
But animals that roam around, are really very nosey

Now Farmer had a fair few goats – well maybe nine or ten
They often ran around the yard, escaping from their pen
They saw the door was open – and thought they'd go and find
Anything that they could eat – that Farmer left behind

Now goats are not too fussy – eating anything they see
With one eating a cushion – and one the Christmas tree
A few were in the kitchen – eating vegetables and fruit
Another in the bedroom started eating Farmers suit

When Farmer got back home again, he really found it shocking
The only bit of Christmas left was half a Christmas stocking
The fairy and a single star were where the tree had stood
And in the kitchen - on the floor - was half a Christmas Pud

"I think that we've been burgled", the farmer sadly feared
Then saw the goat called Hairy Keith - with tinsel in his beard
Another one called Grumpy Stan - had glitter round his eyes
The goats had eaten everything. I guess that's no surprise

"The shops are shut. We need so much.
Where can we get it from?"

"Don't worry" said the Farmers wife,
"there's Santas-sack dot com."

"I'll go online. It will be fine.
They've everything we need."

"It's just as well
on Christmas Eve
with many mouths
to feed."

"I'll help you" said that farmer. "And I need what's on your van"
"The snow is pretty heavy, but I'll get there when I can"
"Thank you" said the driver, "You are oh so very kind"
"I'm stuck about a mile from you. I'm quite easy to find"

"I'm in a big blue parcel van, so not too hard to spot"
"I've got all your Christmas stuff. Your tree, your food, the lot"
Farmer put the phone down, and then ran out to the yard
"I'll take my coat and biggest hat. It's snowing very hard"

It rattled; hissed; and chugged a bit; then gave a mighty clang
It shook quite hard from side to side, gave a whistle and a bang
It popped; it fizzed; and let out smoke – that was so very dense
Then bits fell off, and some shot out
– knocking Ducky off the fence

"It just won't go, and in this snow,
I don't know what we'll do"
"I only have one tractor,
and my car's not working too"
He thought of ways to pull them out
– with something strong of course"
But Bull was on his holidays,
and he couldn't use the horse

Donkey heard and limped away – with a wobble of his knees
Then sat and coughed and sniffed a lot; then gave a little sneeze
"You were well an hour ago, playing football with the Llama"
Donkey smiled a happy smile. He'd just been tricking Farmer

So off they went into the snow, with just the sleigh and rope
They'd have to make it if they could. They were the only hope

They had to change direction twice
as snow had blocked the way
But found the van with driver in,
who said his name was Ray.

They tried to dig the snow away, but the van was really stuck
Then Donkey, Ray, and Farmer pulled but still they had no luck

"It's no use. It won't move at all" said cold and shivering Ray
"It's ok" said the farmer, "Put the parcels in the sleigh"

They loaded up the parcels
and they set off on their way
They couldn't fit them all in
as they needed space for Ray

"We'll come right back and get the rest.
There's no need for alarm"
"And if you're stuck and can't get home,
have Christmas on the farm"

OLD BOGGLES PEAK

The first trip was quite easy,
and they got back really quick.
The second trip was harder
as the snow had fallen thick
"We'll have to go another way.
The road is blocked ahead"
"We'll go around Old Boggles Peak
and down the hill instead"

Old Boggles Peak was up a hill. It was so hard to pull
Though Farmer helped to push a bit – as the sleigh was very full
But going down was harder still – so hard to get some grip
Donkey plodded carefully, but his hooves began to slip.

The sleigh was going much too fast
as down the hill they raced.

His eyes were wide,
his ears were back,
and all four legs were braced.

He wasn't sure how he could stop.
His heart began to pound
With Farmer hanging on behind,
and parcels bouncing round.

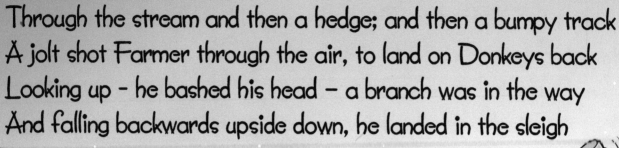

Through the stream and then a hedge; and then a bumpy track
A jolt shot Farmer through the air, to land on Donkeys back
Looking up – he bashed his head – a branch was in the way
And falling backwards upside down, he landed in the sleigh

He struggled to the right way up,
and rubbed his poorly head
And made sure that he held on tight
as down the hill they sped

"I don't think that was Santa. He just cannot go that fast"
The badger and the fox said – as the sleigh went flying past

Farmer started worrying - as they headed for some trees
"Lean to where you want to go, and use your hooves as Ski's"
Donkey leant to his left side. To his surprise he turned
He'd never tried to ski before - but now at last he'd learned

Donkey knew how he could stop, sliding sideways to a halt
A stop so quick caught Farmer out –
which wasn't Donkeys fault

The farmer wasn't hanging on,
and shot out through the air
He landed in the deepest snow,
quite graceful to be fair

He climbed out like a snowman, looking big and round and white
As Donkey laughed – and so did Ray. It was a funny sight
He shook it off and gave a grin. "Wow that was so much fun"
"I'm proud of you young Donkey. You are such a crazy one"

They unpacked all the parcels, and with lots of help from Ray
Started getting Christmas done – but kept the goats away
Not all boxes were for them – things villagers had bought
They put them back inside the sleigh – as Farmer had a thought

"When we've finished working here, I think we should be kind"
"And drop the parcels in the town – if Donkey doesn't mind"
Donkey didn't mind at all. He bounced around with glee
He'd have fun in the snow again. Another chance to Ski

So nice and early the next day - the sun began to rise
The village heard the sound of hooves
- which was a nice surprise

It wasn't Santa's reindeer - though it looked a bit like that
Instead, a happy Donkey - with two antlers on his hat

So, Donkey had saved Christmas,
and 'twas such a special day
Despite the snow the family came,
and joined the fun with Ray

And Donkey told his story - twenty times - then finally
He took the pigs and goats out, and he taught them how to ski

The End

Also available in

The Wobblebottom Farm Series

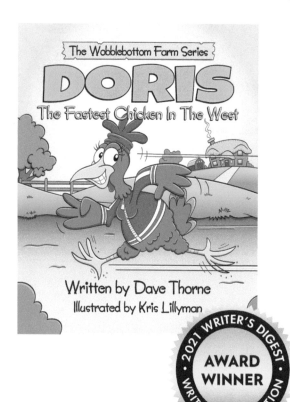

The Wobblebottom Farm Series

DORIS
The Fastest Chicken In The West

Written by Dave Thorne
Illustrated by Kris Lillyman

The Wobblebottom Farm Series

WHEN PIG GOT STUCK IN THE TROUGH

Written by Dave Thorne
Illustrated by Kris Lillyman

2021 WRITER'S DIGEST
AWARD WINNER
WRITING COMPETITION

I wandered down to see the farm, quite late on Christmas Eve
A stunning sight in deepest snow, a land of make-believe

I went to see the Farmer, and saw donkey and the goats
And woolly sheep like fluffy clouds in warmest winter coats

I stopped and had a lovely chat, and many cups of tea
And really liked the Christmas cake, his wife had made for me

But time had come to wander home, as light began to fade
It was a shame I couldn't stay, but fond farewell I bade

As the time changed day to night, and Farmer fell asleep
The only sound was falling snow, on fields so very deep

Then a sound from very near, a strange; surprising noise
I hoped that it was Santa here for all the girls and boys

I looked around excitedly, I'd hoped to see his sleigh
I'd try of course to thank him, just before he flew away

I'd tried since I was very small to stay up just to see
Santa and his reindeer flying round to visit me

I thought the noise had come from in the barn that stored the hay
I really thought it must be him, so close to Christmas Day

So, I crept up very carefully, and peaked around the door
My heart was racing faster than it ever had before

I held my breath excitedly. My heart began to pound.
So, do you think I saw him? Was it Santa that I found?

Nope – it was Donkey falling over an old tin bath in the barn in shock at the
sight of Hairy Keith the goat eating a pair of Farmers old underpants. Disgusting !

Merry Christmas everyone !